A Templar Book

Produced by The Templar Company plc,
Pippbrook Mill, London Road, Dorking, Surrey RH4 1JE, Great Britain.

Text copyright © *Bunny's First Christmas* 1926-1953 by Darrell Waters Limited
Illustration and design copyright © 1993 by The Templar Company plc
Enid Blyton is a registered trademark of Darrell Waters Limited

This edition produced for Parragon Books,
Unit A, Central Trading Estate, Bath Road, Brislington, Bristol.

This book contains material first published as
It's Christmas Time in Enid Blyton's Sunny Stories
and Sunny Stories between 1926 and 1953.

Illustrated by Sue Deakin

Printed and bound in Italy

ISBN 1 85813 319 X

Enid Blyton's

POCKET LIBRARY

BUNNY'S FIRST CHRISTMAS

Illustrated by Sue Deakin

PARRAGON

"It's Christmas time!" said the big rocking horse in the toy shop, one night when the shop was shut, and only the light of the street lamp outside lit up the toys sitting on the shelves and counters.

"What's Christmas?" asked a small bear who had only just arrived.

"Oh, it's a lovely time for children," said the horse, rocking gently to and fro. "They have presents, you know, and Father Christmas comes on Christmas night and fills their stockings with all kinds of toys."

"*You'll* never go into a stocking, rocking horse!" said a cheeky monkey.

"No, I shall stand in somebody's playroom and give them rides," said the horse. "I *shall* look forward to that. I've been here a long time – too long. But I'm very expensive, you know, and people often haven't enough money to buy me."

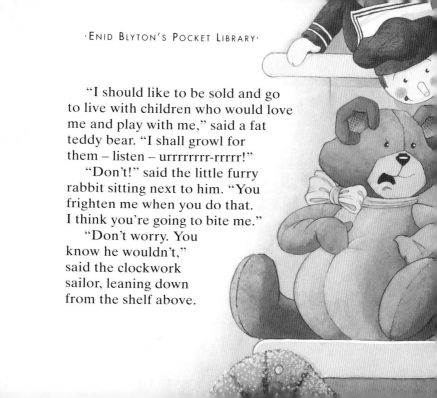

"I should like to be sold and go to live with children who would love me and play with me," said a fat teddy bear. "I shall growl for them – listen – urrrrrrrr-rrrrr!"

"Don't!" said the little furry rabbit sitting next to him. "You frighten me when you do that. I think you're going to bite me."

"Don't worry. You know he wouldn't," said the clockwork sailor, leaning down from the shelf above.

"Come on, Bunny –
let's get down to
the floor and
have a game!"

The rabbit jumped down at once, and the clockwork sailor landed near him. He loved the sailor, who wouldn't let any of the bigger toys tease him or frighten him. Sometimes the pink cat chased him and the little rabbit couldn't bear that!

"Sailor," said the rabbit, when all the toys were playing together. "Sailor, we're friends, aren't we? Sailor, you won't leave me if you are sold and go to live with some children, will you?"

"Well – I shan't be able to help it," said Sailor. "You're my very best friend and I'm yours, and I hope and hope we'll be sold together – but you never know!"

The bunny worried about that, and next day when customers came in and out of the shop, buying this toy and that, the little rabbit hoped that he and the clockwork sailor would be bought by the same person.

But they weren't! An old woman came in and asked for a sailor doll for her grand-daughter whose father was a sailor – and the shop lady at once took down Clockwork Sailor from his shelf.

"He's fine," said the little old woman. "Yes, I'll have him. My grand-daughter Katy will love him! Will you wrap him up for me, please?"

"Goodbye, Sailor!" whispered the little rabbit, sadly. "Oh, I shall miss you so! Goodbye, and be happy!"

Sailor only had time to wave quickly whilst no-one was looking. Then he was wrapped up in brown paper and carried out of the shop, leaving Bunny all by himself. Poor Bunny, he felt lonely and unhappy without his friend by his side. He hoped that the bear wouldn't growl at him or the pink cat chase him.

But that very day he was sold too! A big, smiling woman came in and bought a great many toys at once.

"They're for a Christmas tree," she said. "I am giving a party on Boxing Day for my little girl and her friends, and we've got a perfectly lovely tree to decorate."

"You'll want a pretty fairy doll for the top, then," said the shop lady, pleased. "And what about a little teddy bear and a doll or two?"

"Yes. And I'll have that toy ship – and that wooden engine – and that jack-in-the-box," said the customer. "And I really *must* have that little rabbit – he's sweet!"

Bunny was sold! He couldn't believe it. He was sold at last and would leave the toy shop he knew so well.

Bunny was very pleased to be going with so many other toys he knew. But, oh dear, each of the toys would be given to a different child at the party, so he wouldn't have any friends at all after Boxing Day!

The other toys were terribly excited. It was fun to be sold and leave the toy shop. It would be splendid to be part of the decorations on a beautiful Christmas tree and have crowds of children admiring them. And it would be simply lovely if they were lucky enough to be given to a kind and loving child who would look after and play with them and perhaps even cuddle them in bed.

When they arrived at the smiling lady's house, Bunny was surprised to see such a big Christmas tree. It almost reached the ceiling!

"I don't think I want to be hung up there," he said to the fat teddy bear, who had been sold for the tree too. "I might fall off and hurt myself."

"Don't be such a coward," said the bear. "Ah – here comes someone to see to us! Cheer up, you silly little rabbit and, remember, if you are given to some horrid child, you must just run away and find a new home!"

"Run away? How?"
asked the rabbit, anxiously.
But the bear was very busy
growling at that moment,
because someone
was pressing him in
the middle where
his growl was
kept!

"Urrrr!" he
said proudly.
"Urrrr!"

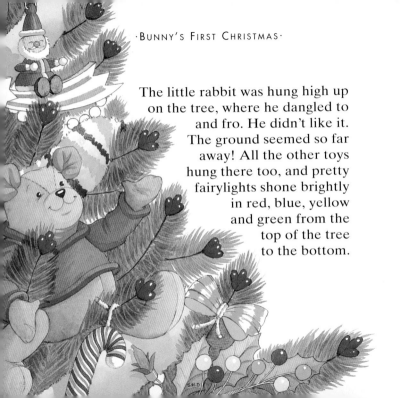

The little rabbit was hung high up on the tree, where he dangled to and fro. He didn't like it. The ground seemed so far away! All the other toys hung there too, and pretty fairylights shone brightly in red, blue, yellow and green from the top of the tree to the bottom.

"The party's tonight!" said a rag doll next to him. "Not long to wait now! Doesn't the fairy look wonderful at the top of the tree?"

Soon the rabbit heard the sound of children's voices and laughter. They were playing games in another room. Then someone came into the big room where the tree stood and switched on all the fairylights again. The tree glowed and shone, and all the pretty ornaments on it glittered brightly. The toys looked lovely as they hung there.

How the children cheered and clapped when they came running in and saw the lovely tree.

"It's beautiful!" they shouted. "Oh, look at the toys! Can you see the fairy doll? Wave your wand, fairy doll, and do some magic!"

"Now, there is a toy for everyone," said the smiling lady who was giving the party. "Harry, here is a ship for you," and she gave him the toy ship. "Lucy, here is a lovely rag doll. I know you want one. Molly, I have just the toy for you – a bear with a growl in his tummy."

Soon there were only a few toys left on the tree. The little rabbit looked down on the children. Was there a little girl called Katy there? The sailor doll had been bought for a Katy. Oh, wouldn't it be wonderful if he was given to her, the same little girl who had Clockwork Sailor?

Who was Bunny going to? He looked and looked at the children. He did hope that he would be given to somebody kind – a nice little girl, perhaps, with a merry face.

"And now, what about a present for *you*, Peter," said the kind lady. "You're not very old – I think you shall have this little furry bunny. Here you are!" So Bunny went to Peter, who held him very tight indeed, and squeezed him to see if he had a squeak inside. But he hadn't.

Bunny didn't like Peter very much, especially when he dropped him on the floor and somebody nearly trod on him.

"Be careful of your little rabbit, Peter," said a big girl.

"I don't like him," said Peter. "I wanted that wooden engine."

Poor little rabbit! He wondered if he could run away, just as the teddy had suggested. He didn't want to go home with Peter. He was sure he was one of the horrid children he had heard spoken about in the toy shop. But he did go home with Peter, and with him went a jigsaw puzzle for Peter's sister.

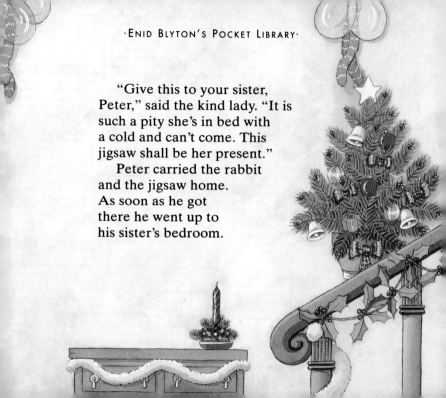

"Give this to your sister, Peter," said the kind lady. "It is such a pity she's in bed with a cold and can't come. This jigsaw shall be her present."

Peter carried the rabbit and the jigsaw home. As soon as he got there he went up to his sister's bedroom.

She was in bed, with a large hanky under her pillow.

"Look – they sent you a jigsaw from the party," said Peter. "And all I got was this silly little rabbit!"

"Oh, Peter – he's sweet!" said the little girl in bed. "I've so many jigsaws – why don't you take this one and I'll have the bunny instead. He shall come into bed with me. He looks rather lonely and, after all, he's only a baby one!"

"All right. I'd much rather have the jigsaw," said Peter. And he threw the rabbit to his sister and went out with the jigsaw underneath his arm.

Bunny landed with a thud on the bed, feeling very sorry for himself. Nothing seemed to be turning out as he had hoped.

The little girl picked him up gently and looked at him.

"Yes, I like you," she said, giving him a hug. "You shall sleep with me at night, so long as you don't mind sharing my bed with another toy. Look, here he is – my very best new toy!"

She pulled back the sheet – and Bunny stared in amazement. He couldn't believe his eyes. Who do you suppose was cuddled down in the bed, looking very happy?

Why, it was Sailor!

Yes, it was the clockwork sailor doll, the one from the toy shop, Bunny's own special friend. Sailor almost sat up in surprise, but just in time he remembered not to. He smiled, though, he smiled and smiled! And so did Bunny!

"I think you like each other," said Katy, because that was her name, of course! "Yes, I'm sure you do. I hope so, anyway, because you've just *got* to be friends." And she gave both of them a happy hug.

"You see, you will sit together on my bed each day, and cuddle down with me at night," she explained, tucking Bunny in beside Sailor.

Katy kissed them both goodnight. Then she lay down, closed her eyes, and was soon fast asleep. And then – what a whispering there was beside her!

"*You!*" said Sailor, in delight. "What a bit of luck!"

"*You!*" said Bunny. "Oh, I can't believe it! What's Katy like?"

"Fine," said Sailor. "You'll love her. Oh, Bunny – what lovely times we're going to have! You'll like the other toys here, too, all except a rude monkey – but I won't let him tease you! Fancy, we shall be able to be friends all our lives now!"

That was three years ago – and they are still with Katy, though they don't sleep with her at night now, because she thinks she's too big for that.

"It *is* nice to have a friend," Bunny keeps saying. Well, it is, isn't it?